# Sofia Makes a Friend

Written by Catherine Hapka
Illustrated by Character Building Studio
and the Disney Storybook Artists

**WWW.ABDOPUBLISHING.COM**

Reinforced library bound edition published in 2015 by Spotlight, a division of ABDO
PO Box 398166, Minneapolis, Minnesota 55439. Spotlight produces high-quality reinforced library
bound editions for schools and libraries. Published by agreement with Disney Enterprises, Inc.

Printed in the United States of America, North Mankato, Minnesota.
052014    072014

 **DISNEP PRESS**
New York

 THIS BOOK CONTAINS
RECYCLED MATERIALS

**CATALOGING-IN-PUBLICATION DATA**

Hapka, Cathy.
 Sofia the first: Sofia makes a friend / Cathy Hapka ; illustrated by Character Building Studio and the
Disney Storybook Artists.
   p. cm. -- (World of reading. Level Pre-1)
Summary: Sofia gets more than she bargained for when a new friend visits the palace!
1. Princesses--Juvenile fiction.  2. Friendship--Juvenile fiction.  3. Crocodiles--Juvenile fiction.  I.
Character Building Studio, ill.  II. Disney Storybook Artists, ill.  III. Title.  IV. Series.
[E]--dc23

978-1-61479-249-9 (Reinforced Library Bound Edition)

**Spotlight**
A Division of ABDO
www.abdopublishing.com

 is excited.
Sofia

Royal visitors are coming

to the  !
palace

2

"King Baldric and Queen Ada
will be here soon," says Queen
Miranda.

"Our visitors are bringing
a special guest," says King Roland.
"I hope you will help her feel at
home in our  ."
palace

"The special guest is probably a princess," Amber whispers to . Sofia

5

A  sounds.

"The guests are here!"  cries.

A  stops in front of the .

trumpet

Sofia

carriage

palace

Two people get out of the .

"Where is the princess?" Amber

wonders.

Then a baby  jumps out of
unicorn

the !
carriage

Queen Ada smiles.

"This is our new pet .
unicorn

Her name is Pearl.

I hope you won't mind watching

her for us."

"Oh!"  cries. "Pearl is so cute!"

Sofia

"Her  is pretty," Amber says.

horn

"It will be fun to watch her!"

Sofia , Amber, and James take Pearl

for a walk.

Pearl chases the  birds and eats

the flowers.

Pearl jumps into the .
fountain

She shakes off next to Amber.

"Hey!" Amber cries. "Stop that!"

"I know," James says.

"Pearl can watch us play ."
horseshoes

He throws a .
horseshoe

Pearl catches the  horseshoe and brings
it back to James.

"Hey! She ruined my throw!"
James says.

Amber has another idea.
"We can play dress-up.

Pearl will look cute in a pretty
hat and tutu."
Pearl takes a big bite
out of Amber's hat.

"No, Pearl!" Amber cries.

She tries to grab the .
hat

But the 🦄 runs away.
unicorn

Pearl runs through the .
palace

She jumps on the and nibbles
piano

on a .
tapestry

"Watching Pearl is no fun," James says.

"She ruins everything," Amber adds.

Pearl hears them talking.

Her head droops. Her  goes dull.
horn

She runs and hides behind a  .
tapestry

"We said we would help Pearl feel at home in our ,"

palace

reminds the others.

Sofia

"But she does not like to do
any of the things we like to do!"
Amber says.

That gives  an idea.
Sofia

"Pearl is a ," she says.
unicorn

"We need to find out what
a  likes to do!"
unicorn

 can hear and talk to animals.

Sofia

 tells Pearl her secret.

Sofia

"What do you like to do?" she asks.

"I love 🎵," says Pearl.

music

25

 leads the   over to where Pearl is hiding. The  play a lively tune.

Sofia     palace     musicians

musicians

, Amber, and James dance and sing along with the ♫.
music

The 🖼 moves. . . .
tapestry

Then Pearl jumps out!
She looks happy, and her pretty
 shines again.

horn

"Hooray!" Sofia cheers.
"We made Pearl feel at home
in our palace."

"Because you figured out what she likes to do."

James smiles at .

"And it's fun for us, too!"

The rest of the visit
is filled with ♫ and fun.
music
, Amber, and James can't wait
Sofia
for Pearl's next visit!